Dear Parent:
Your child's love of readin

Every child learns to read in a different way and at his or her own speed. Some go back and forth between reading levels and read favorite books again and again. Others read through each level in order. You can help your young reader improve and become more confident by encouraging his or her own interests and abilities. From books your child reads with you to the first books he or she reads alone, there are I Can Read Books for every stage of reading:

SHARED READING
Basic language, word repetition, and whimsical illustrations, ideal for sharing with your emergent reader

BEGINNING READING
Short sentences, familiar words, and simple concepts for children eager to read on their own

READING WITH HELP
Engaging stories, longer sentences, and language play for developing readers

READING ALONE
Complex plots, challenging vocabulary, and high-interest topics for the independent reader

ADVANCED READING
Short paragraphs, chapters, and exciting themes for the perfect bridge to chapter books

I Can Read Books have introduced children to the joy of reading since 1957. Featuring award-winning authors and illustrators and a fabulous cast of beloved characters, I Can Read Books set the standard for beginning readers.

A lifetime of discovery begins with the magical words **"I Can Read!"**

Visit www.icanread.com for information on enriching your child's reading experience.

For my cousin Penny,
who doesn't have a mean bone in her body
—J.O'C.

For the truly "nice girls" in my life—you know who you are
—R.P.G.

For M. Girl, who couldn't have been nicer
—T.E.

 For information address HarperCollins Children's Books, a division of HarperCollins Publishers, 10 East 53rd Street, New York, NY 10022.
www.icanread.com

Library of Congress Cataloging-in-Publication Data is available.
ISBN 978-0-06-200178-8 (trade bdg.) — ISBN 978-0-06-200177-1 (pbk.)

11 12 13 14 15 LP/WOR 10 9 8 7 6 5 4 3 ❖ First Edition

by Jane O'Connor

cover illustration by Robin Preiss Glasser

interior illustrations by Ted Enik

HARPER

An Imprint of HarperCollins*Publishers*

This Friday is Field Day.

There are races and a picnic.

Almost everyone is excited.

But one person is dreading it.

(That's fancy for hoping

Field Day never comes.)

That person is me.

Ms. Glass hands out our T-shirts.
I am not on a team
with my friends.
But that is not why I dread Field Day.

I prefer the red T-shirt.

(Prefer means I like it more than mine.)

But that is not why I dread Field Day.

Here is the reason.

I am not a good runner,

and I am in the relay race.

Last year my team lost

because of me.

I got teased.

At recess

Grace is wearing her T-shirt.

It is green.

Oh no! We're on the same team!

Grace can be unkind sometimes.

(That's fancy for mean.)

“I am in the relay race,” Grace tells me.

“Are you?”

I nod.

All Grace says is

“Rats, now we’ll never win!”

At home I see the weather report.

Maybe it will rain.

Then Field Day will be canceled.

(That's fancy for called off.)

But it's going to be sunny and hot. Rats!

Maybe if I practice a lot,

I can get faster by Friday.

Every afternoon I run for hours!

It is no use.

I was born with slow legs.

On Thursday at recess
I hear Grace say,
"I'm stuck in the relay race
with Nancy.
My baby brother runs faster than her."
Isn't that unkind?

At lunch I have no appetite.

(That's means I'm not hungry.)

I don't even finish my cupcake.

Field Day is tomorrow.

I am going to disgrace myself!

(That means I'll look like a fool.)

Lionel is so lucky.

He broke his leg two weeks ago.

He can't be in any races.

Then I get a splendid idea.

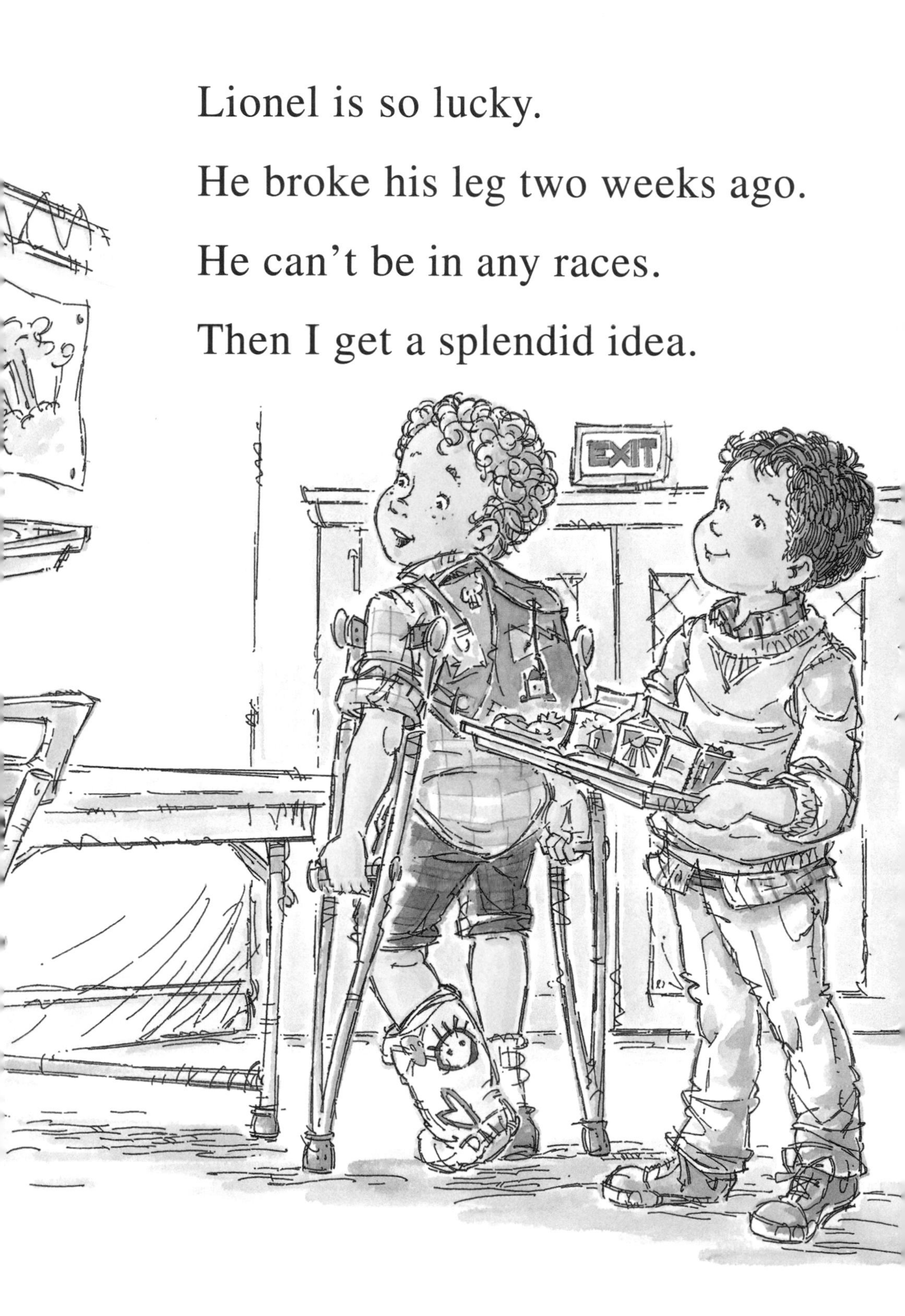

On the way home,
I pretend to trip.
"Ow! Ow!" I say.
"I think I injured my foot."
(Injured is fancy for hurt.)
I limp home.

I limp into the dining room.
My sister helps me to the table.
I tell my parents,
“I don’t think it’s wise for me
to run in the relay race tomorrow.
You’d better write a note.”

Later my dad comes into my room.
"Nancy, is your foot really hurt?"
he asks.
"How can you ask me that?" I say.
My own father doesn't believe me!

So my dad says,

“Well, sometimes you limp on one foot.

And sometimes you limp on the other.”

All of a sudden I start sobbing.
Sobbing is like weeping, only
much more noisy.
I am a bad runner and a fibber!
I tell my dad about the race and Grace.
He understands.
We talk for a long time.

On Field Day I am not limping.

I wear my team T-shirt.

I wear lace-trimmed socks

for good luck.

I cheer for my team.

(I am splendid at cheering.)

Soon it is time for the relay race.

I go up to Grace.

I do not use any fancy words.

"I will run as fast as I can.
But if we lose,
don't say mean stuff.
You are a good runner.
But you are not a good sport."

Grace is speechless!

That means she is so surprised

she can’t say a word.

The relay race starts.

Grace runs all the way to the cone

and then starts back.

She is way ahead of the other runners.

Grace runs back and taps me.

Now I start to run to the cone.

I have a big head start.

But soon the other runners go past me.

I come in last—just like last year.

We lose the race.

I feel so bad!

At the picnic, Grace comes over.

Uh-oh!

But guess what?

All she says is “Want a cookie?

My mom baked them.”

So I say, "*Merci,*" and take one.

And guess what?

My appetite is back!

Fancy Nancy's Fancy Words

These are the fancy words in this book:

Appetite—hungry

Canceled—called off

Disgrace yourself—look like a fool

Dread—not looking forward to something

Injure—hurt

Prefer—like one thing more than another

Sob—noisy weeping

Speechless—too surprised to say a word

Unkind—mean

Wise—smart and understanding